Tales of the Rainbow Forest

Written by McKenzie Willis
with illustrations by Rick Holland

Special thanks to Karen, Cory, Susan and Abby
who helped me bring this story to life.

CONTENTS

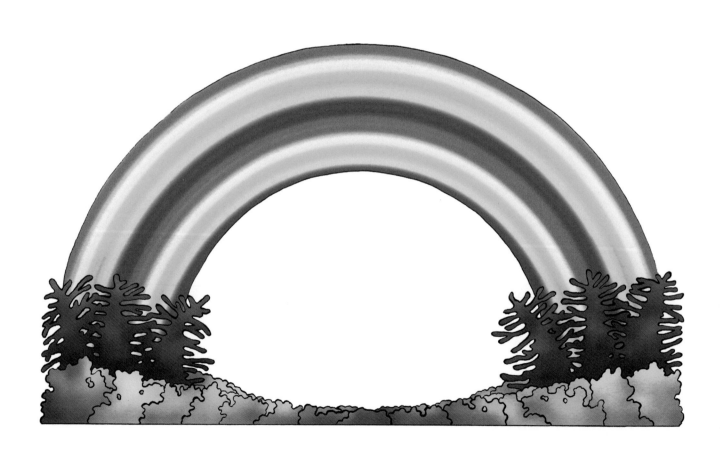

CHAPTER 1
A DAY IN THE RAINBOW FOREST

ONCE UPON A LONG TIME AGO AND FAR FROM WHERE WE ARE NOW, THERE was a beautiful forest. On sunny days it was covered by a sunbeam that made it the brightest of all forests. It was the Rainbow Forest. Many of the forest creatures were unique, like Ida the Spider, who spun webs where colorful butterflies danced.

Yes, that's right, butterflies that dance. You'll see. Everyone knew about the Rainbow Forest, but very few people lived close enough to see who lived there.

Although it was very beautiful, there was one place in the forest that was not safe. It was a scary part and all who lived in the forest stayed away from it. Why was it so scary? Just wait, you'll see!

On some days, puffy rain clouds would slowly sail across the blue sky. When the clouds were above the Rainbow Forest they seemed to stop. Whenever the dwellers, like Ida the Spider, the Busy Bees, and the Silly Salamanders would see these clouds, they would stop whatever they were doing.

The forest would become very quiet. Everyone would begin to smile. Smiles so big that covered their faces because they knew what was about to happen. Soon the clouds would send raindrops falling softly upon the leafy floor.

But those raindrops were not like the ones in all the other forests. They were crystal raindrops.

When the rain began to fall everyone would become very excited. Bees could be heard buzzing, hummingbirds could be heard humming, and butterflies could be heard fluttering their colorful wings. They all knew the crystal raindrops would make the flowers grow bigger with sweeter nectar. The rain also made the forest blueberries the biggest and sweetest of all. The most fun happened near the end of each rainfall. That was when the bright sunbeam would come streaming through the rain clouds. It would cover the whole forest with a big and really beautiful rainbow.

The colors of the raindrops would slowly become the bright red, orange, yellow, green, blue, indigo and violet of the rainbow. That is why they were called crystal raindrops.

Then, sounds of the happy and excited forest dwellers could be heard throughout. The Rainbow Fishes would dart up from the bottom of the pond to blow bubbles at each other. The Silly Salamanders would run so fast while playing their silly games, you could barely see their tiny feet. So, as you can see, rain in the Rainbow Forest was an exciting time for all.

The Sunbeam loved making the Rainbow Forest bright and seeing everyone playing, sharing, and having fun. But, looking down on the forest, the Sunbeam could see one place where there was no one playing or having fun.

"Why?" thought the Sunbeam, "Why is no one there?"

After thinking for a short while, he said, "Ahh... that is the unsafe part. That is where the blueberry fields are."

"Winston the Wicked Dragon lives there, and he wants all the blueberries for himself. He won't SHARE with ANYONE! He spits and breathes hot flames at anyone who comes near." The Sunbeam was not pleased. He wanted everyone to share and have fun in the whole forest.

"Someone has got to stop that wicked dragon from scaring everyone who goes near the blueberry fields," said the Sunbeam. "Who can I find that will make this beautiful forest safe and fun for everyone?" He pondered.

Then suddenly he said, "The Old Man of the Forest, the caretaker for the bees that make Rainbow Forest Honey. No one knows the forest better than he does, except for me," he chuckled. "Now, I just have to find him. I know he's around here somewhere," said the Sunbeam. And sure enough, not far away, underneath a tall tree, the old man lay fast asleep.

Since he'd never spoken to him before, the Sunbeam did not want to frighten him. So he gently blew a feather from a bird's nest that was up in the tree. The feather landed softly on the tip of the old man's

nose. Wiggling his nose and swatting at his face, the old man quickly sat up, with eyes crossed and said, "Wha, wha, what was that?"

"It must have been one of those busy bees again," he said as he struggled to his feet and looked around.

"No, I did it," came a voice from above the treetop.

"What? Who was that? I never heard that voice before!" said the old man.

"You're right. You haven't heard this voice before. It was me," the voice answered.

"Where are you?"

"I'm up here and all over. You see I am the Sunbeam that covers the whole Rainbow Forest."

Looking up, the old man saw a beautiful sunbeam shinning down through the leaves of the tall tree where he had been sleeping.

"Is it really you, Mister Sunbeam? And why did you come to see me?" the old man asked.

"Yes, it's really me," replied the Sunbeam. " I came to see you because I want YOU to be the Keeper of the Rainbow Forest."

"But, I'm just an old Bee-keeper. I can't be the Keeper of this whole big Rainbow Forest," said the old man.

"Oh, yes you can," the Sunbeam said.

"But, I'm not strong enough. How can I?" he asked.

"With MAGIC," answered the Sunbeam. "All MAGIC--that's how you will do it."

"But, I don't know how to do magic," he said to the Sunbeam.

"You will soon," promised the Sunbeam. "On the ground, near where you were sleeping, there is a small branch from the tree."

"There was no branch there before," said the old man.

"There is now," replied the Sunbeam. "Just take a closer look. Do you see it?"

And sure enough, just as the Sunbeam had promised, when the old man looked again, there was a small branch on the ground, right next to where he had been sleeping. With amazement, the old man said, "Yes, yes, I see it now, but it was not there before!"

"Yes I know, but just pick it up," said the Sunbeam.

"But, it's only a small branch," he said as he reached for it.

"Now, what do I do with it?" the old man asked.

"Hold the end of it in one hand and squeeze it quickly three times," advised the Sunbeam.

When the old man squeezed the end of the branch three times, it suddenly became a shiny sword. And from its tip came a quick bright flash of many crystal sparkles. It was brighter than any light anyone had ever seen in the forest before.

"There's more," promised the Sunbeam. "If you look, you will see that you have a silver scabbard on your belt. You now have the one and only Magic Sword in the Rainbow Forest. You should always keep it with you."

Looking down at his belt, the old man saw a beautiful silver scabbard, just as the Sunbeam had said. The old man was now even more amazed than before. "How, how did you do that?" he asked the Sunbeam.

"Magic," answered the Sunbeam. "It's all magic."

"Now that you have the Magic Sword, you have the power. I am making you the Keeper of the Rainbow Forest. Remember, you must always keep the Magic Sword with you. And whenever there is trouble in the forest, just take the sword from your silver scabbard, point it at the trouble, and quickly squeeze it three times," said the Sunbeam.

"How will I know when there's trouble, or where it is?" asked the new Keeper of the Rainbow Forest.

"With the Magic Sword at your side you will always know when and where there's trouble in the Rainbow Forest. And, there IS going to be trouble. Well, I have other work to do. Good luck Keeper of the Rainbow Forest."

And, quick as a flash, the Sunbeam went soaring back up to the sky.

CHAPTER 2
IN A BACK YARD IN SNOGARD

FLUTTER THE BUTTERFLY LIVED IN THE RAINBOW FOREST, BUT WOULD OFTEN leave to find nectar and flowers in other places. On this early morning the butterfly sailed into a backyard in the small village of Snogard, which was not far from the Rainbow Forest. There were many flowers in a garden and a big cherry tree in the yard. Benny and his younger sister Ellie loved playing in their backyard. One day, while playing under the cherry tree, they suddenly saw a shadow darting about on the ground. When they looked up to see what was causing the shadow, a butterfly quickly sailed past them.

"Look, Benny," said Ellie excitedly. "It's a butterfly. Can you see it?"

"Yes," whispered Benny. They watched as the biggest, most beautiful butterfly they had ever seen sailed over and gently landed on a blossom of a low branch of the cherry tree.

They both loved watching and chasing butterflies. Benny whispered to Ellie, "Let's try and get closer to it. We might be able to catch it."

"We could never get close enough to catch that big butterfly. He's too fast," said Ellie.

"Shh, if we're quiet, we might be able to sneak up on it," Benny said.

Moving quietly and slowly, they got very close. They were so close they could see the black spots on its large yellow wings. Just as Benny was about to reach out to catch it, the butterfly flew away. It landed on one of the big yellow sunflowers, which grew along the path leading into a wooded area.

They again moved quietly and slowly, getting closer to the butterfly as it sat on the sunflower. This time they got even closer than they did before. Benny slowly moved his hand near the very tip of the butterfly's wings, and quickly tried to catch it. Just as he touched the tip of one of its wings, the butterfly fluttered away, going farther down the lane into the woods.

After trying for a very long time to catch the butterfly, Ellie said to her brother, "I'm too tired to chase it any more. Can we rest for just a little while?"

"Yes," answered Benny. "I'm tired too. Let's sit here and nap for a little while."

Without realizing it, they had wandered into the Rainbow Forest. They sat down and leaned against a large boulder that was on the side of the lane. They were so tired from chasing the butterfly they soon fell fast asleep as the butterfly sailed farther into the forest.

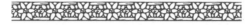

CHAPTER 3
TROUBLE IN THE RAINBOW FOREST

A S THEY LAY SLEEPING, A BREEZE BEGAN TO STIR. AT FIRST IT WAS GENTLE, but then it became stronger. It was no longer a cool gentle breeze. It became quite warm, and then it was hot. It was so hot it started heating up the boulder Benny and Ellie were leaning against.

Awakened by the heat, Ellie asked, "Why is it so hot?"

Before Benny could answer, they heard a loud voice. It was so loud it shook the large boulder.

"What are you doing here?" roared the voice.

Benny and his sister were very, very frightened. When they looked up, they saw a huge dragon. It stood nearly as tall as some of the forest trees.

Again the dragon roared, "What are you doing here?" This time, as he spoke, Benny and Ellie could see his fiery red tongue, and the hot flames coming from his nose as he breathed.

"We... we were just resting, because we were chasing a big butterfly and got really tired," said Ellie, as tears rolled down her cheeks.

"And while we were resting, we fell asleep," said her brother.

"Yeah, yeah, chasing butterflies, getting tired, and falling asleep," shouted the dragon. "I've heard that story before. Don't try to fool me. Do you know who I am?"

Before either of them could answer, he roared in a voice even louder than before. "I am Winston the Wicked Dragon. And I know you are here to try to steal my blueberries from the blueberry field."

"But, but we were just resting here," whimpered Ellie.

"BE QUIET and listen to me," ordered the Wicked Dragon, as the hot flames came even closer to the frightened children. "This is MY part of the forest. These are MY blueberries, and I share with NO ONE! Anyone who tries to steal them gets into big trouble with me."

"But we didn't know we were in your part of the forest. We didn't know there were blueberries here. We wouldn't steal ANYTHING from ANYONE," cried Benny.

"Could you please let us go home?" begged Ellie.

"Quiet, while I think of what I'm going to do with you two," roared the dragon. He started moving slowly towards them, as the flames from his big nostrils got hotter and hotter.

"Benny, I'm so scared. I want to go home now," cried Ellie.

"I'm scared, too," whispered her brother, now holding his sister's hand.

As they stood there frightened and waiting, they heard footsteps coming from behind them. Looking back, they saw an old man. He was holding something in his hand.

"Who are you sir, and what is that you are holding in your hand?" asked Benny, even more afraid.

Knowing how frightened they were, the old man assured them, "Don't worry, you are in the Rainbow Forest and I am the Keeper here. I am here to help you and your sister."

Hearing the Keeper tell Benny and his sister that he was there to help them, the Wicked Dragon sneered, "So, who are you, another thief trying to steal my blueberries?"

"No, Winston," answered the old man. "First of all, no one is here to steal anything, and second of all, these are NOT your blueberries. I am the Keeper of the Rainbow Forest, and I'm here to make the forest safe for everyone to share and have fun."

"Keeper of the Rainbow Forest," growled the angry dragon. "What a joke. All three of you are going up in smoke." he said as he took a deep breath to blow hot flames at them.

"Winston, I am warning you! You are about to make a big mistake, and you will be very, very sorry if you don't stop right now." promised the Keeper, as he began to raise the Magic Sword.

"You're just a little old man, and you don't tell ME what to do." commanded the dragon, as he began to blow hot flames at them.

The Keeper pointed the Magic Sword at the hot flames, and quickly squeezed it three times, sending bright crystal sparkles speeding through the air. The speed of the sparkles was so fast they crashed into the dragon's hot flames, and sent them back up his nose and made him sneeze. They made him sneeze so hard; he went flying backwards, up and over the treetops, above the clouds, and out of sight.

As Winston the Wicked Dragon disappeared through the clouds, everyone throughout the Rainbow Forest could hear a loud "Aaahhhhhchooooo!" It was hard for Ellie and Benny to believe that the crystal sparkles could make the wicked dragon sneeze himself completely out of sight!

"How, how did you do that?" asked Ellie, as she and Benny stood looking beyond the treetops.

"MAGIC," answered the Keeper of the Rainbow Forest. He smiled as he looked at his magic sword. "It's all magic."

"Now then," he said. "let's get going you two. There is a lot for you to see and do while you're here in the Rainbow Forest."

"But what if Winston the Wicked Dragon comes back?" Benny asked.

"You don't have to be afraid. The Wicked Dragon will not be coming back," promised the Keeper. "So, just have fun while you are here."

As they walked down the lane, the Old Man looked up and whispered, "How did I do?"

"Very well, very well indeed," answered the Sunbeam softly. "I'm very proud of you, Keeper of the Rainbow Forest."

Ellie and Benny began their walk in the beautiful forest. They soon noticed a few leaves moving on the ground. Some moved slowly while others moved very quickly.

"Why are the leaves moving?" Ellie asked her brother, but before he could answer, she said, "Look at that one. It looks like it's running. Do these leaves have feet? The leaves in our yard don't move like this."

"Yes, I know," said Benny. "But leaves don't have feet Ellie. Let's see if we can get a closer look at them. Maybe we can see why some are moving."

Soon after kneeling on the ground, they saw something that made them laugh right out loud. What they saw were beautiful yellow salamanders. It seemed like they were playing silly salamander games as they ran around underneath the leaves.

They watched them play their silly games for a while. Then they continued on their walk, farther down the winding path.

They were laughing at how funny the salamanders were, when suddenly they came upon a very big spider web. As they were looking at the big web, a voice said, "Hello!"

As Ellie and Benny looked around to see who spoke to them, they heard the voice say again. "Hello!"

This time, they saw something waving to them from the edge of the large web. It was a spider sitting between two sparkling dewdrops.

"Hello! Who are you?" said Benny, surprised to see that a spider could talk.

"My name is Ida-the-Spider; I spin special webs."

"Why is your web so big?" asked Ellie.

But before Ida-the-Spider could answer, a butterfly fell into her web.

"That's why," said Ida, pointing at the butterfly, who was now struggling in the web.

Afraid for the butterfly, Benny cried, "No, no! Don't eat the butterfly. That's the one we were chasing before we got lost here in the Rainbow Forest."

"Now, now, don't worry. I will not eat the butterfly," promised the spider. "The web is big and strong. It's a safe place for the butterfly to be."

"It can't fly away now. How can the web be safe?" asked Ellie.

"Well, come closer, and I will tell you," said Ida, as she moved closer to the edge of her web. "Do you see that honeysuckle bush just above my web?"

"Yes," said Benny. "I see it. It has flowers on it."

"Yes," said the spider. "The flowers on that bush have very sweet nectar in them. Butterflies love to drink honeysuckle nectar. It's a special treat for them. Because it's so good, sometimes they drink too much of it and they get too full. Then, when they try to fly away, they just fall down into my special web, and do funny dances as they try to free themselves."

"That's mean, Ida," said Ellie.

"Is that what happened to this butterfly? Did it drink too much nectar?" asked Benny.

"Yes," answered the spider. "But don't worry. Just watch what happens."

Sure enough, just as Ida said, the butterfly struggled to free itself from the web, and started to do funny dances. It tipped from side to side and bounced up and down on the web.

While this was happening, Ida began to laugh. Pretty soon, Ellie and Benny began laughing also because the dance was really funny. After struggling for so long the exhausted butterfly tipped over on its side.

Finally, Ida stopped laughing. She slowly moved over to one of the shiny crystal dewdrops on her web. With her feet, she began to roll the dewdrop over to where the butterfly was lying on the sticky web.

Seeing what Ida-the-Spider was doing, Benny and Ellie stopped laughing and became very quiet. They were both afraid of what was about to happen to the beautiful butterfly.

As Ida gave the dewdrop one last push, it slowly rolled underneath the butterfly's feet. As soon as the dewdrop touched the butterfly's feet, it popped up and it started to dance gracefully all over Ida's web.

After dancing for a while the butterfly stopped, and like a ballet dancer, took a bow as if to say thank you to Ida-the-Spider. Then it flew high and away through the Rainbow Forest.

"What happened?" asked Ellie. "Did the dewdrop free the butterfly?"

"Yes, it did," answered Ida.

"But why did it dance that way? Butterflies can't dance," Benny said.

"Magic... It's all magic in the crystal dewdrop," explained Ida-the-Spider.

CHAPTER 4
BUSY BEES

WHILE ELLIE AND BENNY WERE HAVING FUN IN THE FOREST, THE dragon was floating in the clouds high above. He couldn't see the forest and was very cold, because he no longer had his fire to keep him warm.

He was also very hungry and lonely. More than anything, he wished he could be back in the beautiful Rainbow Forest. He began to cry big dragon tears.

"Why are you crying, Winston?" asked the Sunbeam.

"I'm crying because I am cold, hungry, and very tired. I can't stop floating, and I'm very lonely. I wish I could go back," said Winston.

"Could you please help me to go back?"

"The only way you can return to the Rainbow Forest is if the Keeper lets you come back," answered the Sunbeam.

"Could you please, please ask him to let me come back? I would always share with everyone and never scare anyone ever again," the dragon begged.

"Well," said the Sunbeam, "I will speak with the Keeper of the Rainbow Forest, and tell him what you promised, but I don't know if he will ever let you come back, Winston," said the Sunbeam.

"Oh, thank you sir," said the dragon. "When will you ask the Keeper of the Forest?"

But the Sunbeam just disappeared, without answering the sad dragon. Back in the forest, Benny and Ellie were walking past fields of daisies and other colorful flowers. They saw many of the dwellers playing and having fun. But they noticed that the bees were not playing, and they did not look like they were having fun. They were busy dipping their noses in the purple clover.

"Why are the bees so busy?" asked Ellie, "They should be playing and having fun like everyone else."

Before Benny could answer, the Keeper of the Forest, who was standing close by, said, "Those bees are the worker bees. They are the collectors of nectar from the flowers. They don't have time to play and have fun."

"What do they do with it when they collect it?" asked Benny. "Does it make them do funny dances like the butterflies do after they collect nectar from the honeysuckle flowers?"

"No, no, not at all," answered the Keeper. "They take it to the hive."

"Then what happens to it?" Ellie wanted to know.

"The worker bees make sweet Rainbow Forest Honey," explained the Keeper.

"Oh," said Ellie. "Could we have a taste of it?"

"No, not just yet, they are much too busy. When the nectar has been turned to honey, you might be able to have a taste of it," said the Keeper.

As they walked farther down the lane, a buzzing sound could be heard.

"What is that sound? Where is it coming from?" Ellie asked.

"Look, look, it's coming from over there," exclaimed Benny, as he pointed at a swarm of bees not far from where they were standing.

Both Benny and Ellie were so excited. They asked the Keeper of the Rainbow Forest if they could go over to get a closer look at the bees. Seeing how excited Ellie and her brother Benny were, the Keeper knew he had to explain something to them.

"First of all, began the Keeper, "There is something you both need to know". When you see a swarm of bees, there is usually a hive. They are worker bees and they collect nectar to make honey. They also protect the hive and the busy queen bee who is laying hundreds of eggs. The eggs will become new bees to help make sweet honey. Black bears search for bee hives to steal the honey that is inside. Worker bees think that anything that is black is a bear coming to steal the honey. The worker bees will defend their queen's hive by using the only weapon they have – their stingers."

Ellie and Benny were wearing black shirts, so the Keeper advised them not to go near the hive, because the bees might think they are bears and sting them.

"To be safe, both of you need to be wearing white shirts and white hats with netting to keep the bees from stinging you," said the Keeper.

"But we don't have hats with netting. We only have the shirts we're wearing," said Benny, sadly.

"We're not going to see the bees making honey!" cried Ellie.

The Keeper began to think. Suddenly, he remembered something. "Ahh, the Magic Sword," he said softly to himself.

He gently pulled the sword from the silver scabbard on his belt, squeezing it three times. Sparkles floated around Ellie and Benny. When the sparkles were gone, they were each wearing a white shirt and a hat with netting. They could NOT believe what they were seeing.

"Ellie!" said Benny. "You are wearing a white shirt and a hat with netting now!"

"So are you," said Ellie, excitedly. "How did you do that?" she asked the Keeper.

"Magic, it's all magic," he answered as he looked up and winked quickly at the Sunbeam. "Now," he said, "let's take a closer look at the hive to see if we can get a look at the busy bees making Rainbow Forest Honey."

After quietly watching the busy bees as they worked very hard at making honey, the Keeper whispered to Benny and his sister, "It seems the bees are too busy to let you taste the honey, now. Maybe if we come back later, they will let you have a taste of it. Come," said the Keeper. "There is still much more to see."

After walking down the lane for a while with the Keeper, there came a sweet smelling breeze from behind them. It was one of the worker bees and the sweet breeze was from the honeycombs it was carrying.

It gently placed a small honeycomb on Ellie and Benny's shoulders, winked at them and flew back to the hive. "I really like the crown it was wearing. Was that the queen?" asked Ellie. "No, answered The Keeper. The queen could not leave the hive, but she likes you two so she let the worker bee use her crown."

Ellie and Benny were very surprised and happy. They had their first taste of sweet Rainbow Forest Honey and oh, was it good! Yum, Yum, it was the BEST! They happily walked along the lane with the Keeper, licking the yummy honey from their sticky fingers.

CHAPTER 5
WHERE IS WINSTON?

IN THE MEANTIME, HIGH ABOVE THE RAINBOW FOREST, WINSTON THE WICKED Dragon was still floating among the clouds. There were many more clouds now and they were much darker than they were when the Keeper first cast him out of the forest with his Magic Sword. The dragon was so tired he could barely keep his eyes open, or speak. He just wanted to lie down and sleep, but he couldn't, because he couldn't stop floating. As he was floating around and becoming more and more tired, the Sunbeam started to slowly shine through the dark clouds.

"Oh, there you are," said the dragon softly. "It's so good to see you. Did you speak with the Keeper about letting me come back?"

"Yes, I did," answered the Sunbeam. "He said you can come back, but..."

Winston the Dragon was so excited that he didn't let the Sunbeam finish.

"Oh, thank you, sir, thank you. When can I go back? When, when?"

"Wait, Winston. Not so fast. There are a few things you need to know before the Keeper will let you come back into the Rainbow Forest."

"Tell me! Tell me quickly, because I'm hungry, cold, and very tired," the dragon pleaded.

"QUIET Winston," demanded the Sunbeam. "You have to listen to me. Listen carefully, or you will NEVER be allowed to come back. And I'm only going to tell you these things once," warned the Sunbeam.

"I'm sorry, sir. I'm just so excited. I'll be quiet and listen to everything you say," promised the dragon.

"Now then," said the Sunbeam. "First of all, if you're allowed to return to the Rainbow Forest, you can never, ever scare anyone again. You must share with everyone, AND, you'll have to be especially kind to Benny and his sister Ellie, and do something special for them."

"And Winston," said the Sunbeam. "You will NOT be allowed to be a dragon in the Rainbow Forest! Do you understand what I am saying to you?"

"Yes sir," answered the dragon. "I understand, but could you please tell me when the Keeper of the Forest will let me return? And what AM I going to be?"

But the Sunbeam did not answer, as he quickly disappeared above the clouds.

"Where...where are you? Where did you go?" asked the dragon, as he tried to find the Sunbeam. But there was still no answer—only silence.

Then, the clouds started to get very dark and it got very windy. The winds blew so strongly that they stopped the dragon's floating, and began to spin him around in circles. There was a loud sound, much louder than thunder. As the winds swirled around him, he suddenly began to fall very fast down through the dark clouds.

The dragon became so frightened he closed his eyes, because he did not want to see where he was falling. It was too scary for him to watch and he kept falling until finally, there was a loud splash.

He was no longer falling, but he was still afraid, so he kept his eyes closed tightly. For a while there was complete silence. Not a sound could be heard anywhere!

Finally, Winston very slowly opened his eyes. "Where am I?" he said softly.

"You are on the bottom of a pond," came a voice from the water's edge.

"Who, who are you? Why am I in a pond?" asked Winston. "I don't know how to swim. Dragons don't live in water."

"Winston, you MUST understand this," answered the voice from the water's edge. "You are no longer a dragon. You are back in the Rainbow Forest."

"Ahh, you must be the Keeper of the Rainbow Forest that the bright Sunbeam told me about," said Winston, excitedly. "Thank you so much for letting me come back. I missed being here very much. I want to stay forever. I am very hungry. Is there anything I can eat?" "Yes," answered the Keeper. "You can eat water bugs and other small pond-creatures, if you can catch them."

"Little bugs and small pond-creatures? They could NEVER fill me up," said Winston.

"Winston," repeated the Keeper, "you are not a dragon anymore. And you are not as big as you were before. Some of the pond-critters are bigger than you are."

After taking a long look at himself, Winston said in a very sad voice, "My tail! I don't have a long tail anymore! My legs are short, and I'm sooo ugly."

He looked at the Keeper, who was now standing closer and asked, "What am I?"

"For now you are a pond nymph," answered the Keeper. "And yes, you are quite ugly. But you won't be when you grow up."

"What will I be when I'm all grown up?" Winston asked the Keeper.

"You will become a Dragonfly."

"A Dragonfly," repeated Winston. "Will I be able to fly?"

"Yes, you will be able to fly."

"Oh, great," said Winston. "A dragon that flies."

"No, no, Winston!" said the Keeper firmly. "Listen to me. I said you could NEVER be a dragon again in this forest. Do you understand that?"

"Yes, I understand. I'm sorry. I won't ever call myself a dragon again."

"Good. Now, I must warn you, it will not be easy for you growing up to be a Dragonfly. But if you do as I tell you, it CAN be done."

"I will do everything you tell me to do," promised Winston. "I NEVER want to be cast out of the Rainbow Forest again."

"So listen to me carefully," said the Keeper. "Many of the pond-critters are bigger than you are, and they are just waiting for something to eat. They could swallow you up in one big gulp."

The thought of being eaten by one of the pond-critters made Winston more afraid than ever before. The Keeper told him to hide underneath a stone and quietly wait for water bugs or other pond-critters that were smaller than he. When one of the critters came close enough to where he was hiding, the Keeper told him to quickly dart out, grab it, and then hurry back to his hiding place to eat it.

Even though he was more afraid than he'd ever been before, Winston wanted more than anything to grow up to be a Dragonfly in the Rainbow Forest. So he promised he would wait underneath a stone for something to catch for food.

As the Keeper began to walk away from the water's edge, he stopped and looked at Winston. He said, "Good luck, Winston. I hope you are a Dragonfly the next time I see you."

Then without waiting for a reply, he disappeared down the Rainbow Forest lane.

Chapter 6
Where are Ellie and Benny?

A FTER WALKING DOWN THE LANE FOR A LONG TIME, THE KEEPER BECAME very thirsty, so he walked over to get a drink of water from the flowing spring. After having a nice cool drink, he sat down to rest for a while. As he sat there he wondered, "Where are Ellie and Benny?"

Just as he asked himself the question, he heard their voices as they walked past him along the forest's tree-lined path. They were so busy looking at all the Rainbow Forest Creatures, and flowers they never saw him. Seeing them having so much fun brought a big smile to his face. He was quite pleased. After walking for a while, Benny and Ellie heard a sound they had not heard before in the forest.

"Where is that sound coming from, Benny?" Ellie asked.

"I don't know, said Benny, but it's getting much louder. It sounds like it's coming from above."

They both looked up and there before them, was a waterfall streaming down the mountainside into a little pond. They walked to the edge of the pond and stood there. After standing there for a while, they noticed something was moving about very quickly in the water.

"Benny, what is that moving in the water?"

"I don't know. It's moving so fast, I can't see what it is," said Benny.

"Maybe we could see it if we get a little closer," said Ellie, as she began to move closer to the edge of the pond.

"Okay, but wait," said Benny, as he grabbed his sister's hand. "Don't get too close to the water because something might pull you in."

Just as they moved closer, a silvery fish came to the surface. Its tail splashed them with water. Surprised, they both jumped back and began laughing as they wiped the cool water from their face.

"Aahhh," said Ellie. "The water feels so good. I wish we could go into the pond just for a little while."

Just at that time, another fish jumped higher out of the water and splashed them with even more water than the one before. He said to them, "Take off your shoes; come in and play in our pond."

Ellie and Benny were so excited they quickly took their shoes off, but walked slowly into the water. The fish that had splashed them with the most water said, "Welcome to our pond!" Then he splashed them again.

"What kind of fish are you?" Benny asked.

"We are the Rainbow Fish," he answered, while doing a big backwards flip in the water.

"We've never seen Rainbow Fish before," said Ellie.

"That's because we're the very special fish of the Rainbow Forest. We are the only fish in this pond."

While splashing Ellie and Benny again, the fish said, "Come on you two! Let's have some pond fun. We're going to play the Pond Bubble game."

"What kind of game is that? How do you play it?" Benny asked.

"Just wait, you'll soon see," answered the fish.

Suddenly many Rainbow Fish came swimming over and began splashing and darting through the water. One of them blew a big beautiful bubble. With its tailfin, he batted the bubble over to another fish that was swimming near him. That fish then batted it to another and soon they were all batting and blowing the big bubble around. One of the fish batted the bubble to Ellie. She caught it and threw it to her brother, who threw it to the big fish that had asked them to join and play the Pond Bubble game.

They had all been playing and having fun for a long time when Benny suddenly stopped, and yelled to his sister. "Ellie, Ellie! Look over there!"

"What is it? What are you looking at?" Ellie asked as she moved quickly through the water to be near her brother.

"Something ugly and scary looking just came from underneath that stone and chased a tiny frog," said Benny.

As they stood quietly watching, the ugly critter again darted quickly out from underneath the stone. This time, it grabbed a water bug and scampered back underneath the stone. Seeing this, Ellie became frightened, and said, "We'd better get out of the water. It looks mean and has a very big mouth. Let's hurry! It might come after us, too."

They quickly waved goodbye to their Rainbow Fish friends, and were about to leave when a voice softly called to them, "Stay in the water, please. You don't have to leave."

"Was that one of the Rainbow Fish saying that?" Ellie asked.

"No, it was me," came the voice again.

"Oh, it was that ugly creature," said Benny, as he pointed at the stone.

"Don't worry," came the soft voice again. "You don't need to be afraid of me. I know I'm ugly and I look scary, but I won't harm you. I promise! It makes me so sad that you are afraid of me."

"What are you?" Benny asked. Why did you chase that tiny frog and eat that water bug?"

"For now, I am a pond nymph, but not for long. I hope to become a grownup real soon. But to become a grownup, I have to eat a lot of food," said the Ugly Nymph.

"Once I'm all grown up, I will become one of the special Rainbow Forest dwellers. So, if you don't leave, you will see something amazing, get a special treat, and I will be your friend for a long, long time," the nymph promised. No longer afraid, Benny and Ellie returned to splash around and play the Pond Bubble game with their Rainbow Fish friends.

CHAPTER 7
THE UGLY POND NYMPH BECOMES A DRAGONFLY

AFTER PLAYING WITH THE FISH FOR A WHILE, BENNY SAID TO HIS SISTER, "Let's go and see if the Ugly Nymph is still there." They were quite surprised at what they saw. The nymph had grown much bigger. It was struggling to climb onto a fallen branch that was at the edge of the pond. Just as he was about to finish his climb, he slipped and fell back into the pond. A hungry swan flying above the pond saw the falling nymph and quickly sailed down to go after it.

When Ellie and Benny saw the swan going after the nymph, they both yelled, "No, no, no! Don't eat the nymph!"

The swan was frightened by their loud yells, and it flew away, high above the forest trees. The nymph thanked them for saving him from being eaten by the swan. After resting for a short time, the nymph tried again to climb onto the branch. It was very hard to do, but he had to keep trying because he had to get out of the water and into the sun. Finally, he was able to climb onto the branch and stay there, but he was very tired and needed to rest for a little while.

Ellie and Benny watched very closely as he lay there in the sun. Once the nymph was rested and dry, they saw something they COULD NOT BELIEVE. Two very large eyes began to slowly grow through the skin on top of the nymph's head. Then, with much more struggling, three legs grew slowly through the skin on each side of his body. He was again very tired, but he was not finished yet. He could not stop to rest; he had to hurry, because that hungry swan might come back to eat him.

As Benny and Ellie watched, something very strange happened. The nymph let out a startled cry as something began to grow through the skin on his back! When it was finished growing, they could see

it was a tail. Then four iridescent wings came through, two on each side. They were very wide and long. But, he was still not finished. With his six strong legs, and his four long wings, he began to push and pull, pull and push, until with one final pull, he was free from the old UGLY skin that had covered him.

He looked at himself, smiled, and winked at Ellie and Benny with one of his big eyes. Then he flew high above the pond, up and down, sideways, and in circles, before landing on the ground right next to Ellie and Benny.

"Well, everything works!" he said. "Hello Ellie and Benny; my name is Winston the Dragonfly and I want to be your new friend."

"You are a dragon that flies?" asked Ellie.

"No, no," said Winston. "I am a dragon-FLY. NOT a dragon! Do you remember when you were chasing that big colorful butterfly and got so tired you had to stop to rest, but then fell asleep?"

"Yes," said Ellie. "We remember."

"Well, I was that fire-spitting wicked dragon that was so mean to you."

"Oh yes," said Benny, "I remember. The Keeper of the Rainbow Forest made you disappear with the Crystal Sparkles from his Magic Sword. YOU were that wicked dragon?"

"Yes, that's right," agreed Winston the Dragonfly. "The Keeper would not let me return to the Rainbow Forest as a dragon. I had to promise Mr. Sunbeam that I would share with everyone and NEVER, EVER scare anyone again. Only then was I allowed to come back. It's sooo good to be back as a dragonfly. I would like to sincerely apologize to you for scaring you when I was a wicked dragon"

FUN FACT

Did you know that dragonflies fly up to 30 miles per hour?

CHAPTER 8
A SPECIAL DRAGONFLY TREAT

WINSTON THE DRAGONFLY THANKED ELLIE AND BENNY FOR NOT running away when he was the Ugly Nymph and for staying to see him grow up.

"I really want to be one of your Rainbow Forest friends," said Winston the Dragonfly. "Now it's time for that special treat I promised you."

"What is it? What is it?" Benny asked excitedly.

"Yes!" said Ellie. "We want to know what the special treat is."

"Well," said Winston, "there is a place here in the forest where there are sweet and juicy blueberries growing. And they are just waiting to be eaten by two very hungry little people."

"Ooohh, that sounds good," said Ellie. "We LOVE blueberries. How do we get there?"

"That will be very easy," answered the Dragonfly. "All you have to do is just climb onto my back and I will fly you there."

"But you might not be strong enough to fly with both of us on your back," said Ellie.

"I have four very strong wings. I can fly high, low, and fast. I can even fly backwards. So, if you want to get to those blueberry fields, you'd better hurry and climb on board," said the Dragonfly. They were both very excited. Benny helped Ellie climb on first. Then he quickly, but carefully climbed on.

"Is everybody ready to fly?" called out Winston.

"Yes, we are!" they answered.

At first, Winston's wings began to move slowly, then faster, and suddenly they were flying.

"We're flying! We're flying!" Benny shouted to his sister.

"Yes, and it's so much fun. We can see the Rainbow Forest below," yelled back Ellie.

While flying high above the forest trees, Winston saw the white swan that had wanted to eat him when he was the Ugly Nymph in the pond. He watched the swan for a while, before he suddenly realized that he had flown past the blueberry fields. Knowing that Ellie and Benny would be surprised and very excited, he began to fly very slowly, then stopped, and with his wings still moving, he hovered above the trees just beyond the edge of the blueberry fields.

"Benny, Benny, look, we're standing still, but we are still in the air," said Ellie, excitedly.

"Yes, I know," said Benny. "This is so much fun. How are you doing this Winston?"

But Winston would only say, "This is all part of the special treat I promised you. Just wait; there's more. You both will need to hold on tightly for this one."

He suddenly began to fly backwards until they were high above the blueberry fields again.

Winston said as he slowed down, "You don't have to hold on so tightly now, if you look down, you'll see that we are above the blueberry fields at last."

He then started to fly downward in a series of circles, and he even circled around the white swan. The swan waved hello to them with one of his big white wings as they flew past him. First of all, Benny and Ellie were very excited to be flying in circles; but circling around the swan and saying hello to it was even more exciting. After saying hello they watched as the swan sailed away. They looked down and saw that they were close enough to see the blueberry fields.

Then before they landed something happened that Benny could hardly believe. "Ellie," he whispered in his sister's right ear. "A butterfly just landed on your left shoulder." Not wanting to scare the butterfly away, Ellie turned her head slowly to look. Sure enough, sitting there on her shoulder was a butterfly.

"Oh Benny," she whispered, "It's the same one we chased down the lane."

"Yes, you're right. And it's the same one that was dancing on Ida's spider web," said Benny.

The butterfly stayed on Ellie's shoulder for a short time. Then it did a little dance and sailed down to the honeysuckle bush above Ida the Spider's web. This all made Winston the Dragonfly very, very happy, because he KNEW this was the butterfly Ellie and Benny were chasing before he scared them with his hot

flames, when he was a wicked dragon. It felt so good to be having fun with them now. They were now close enough to the blueberry bushes to see the berries.

"Okay," Winston said to them. "We are almost there. If you look down you can see those big juicy berries just waiting for two hungry people. We're about to go in for a landing. Hold on tight."

Winston began to slowly sail down. At last he landed softly, right next to a bush that had more blueberries than any other berry bushes. Benny climbed off first; then he helped Ellie. They began eating the berries. They were delicious! They thanked Winston for bringing them to the bush with the sweetest and juiciest blueberries of all.

"Don't you want to eat some berries, too?" Benny asked Winston. "They are sooo good!"

"No, thank you," answered Winston. "I can see there are many mosquitoes flying around here, and I love mosquitoes. So, while you are eating blueberries, I'll be chasing and eating mosquitoes. But I'll be here when you're finished and ready to leave."

Dragonflies do love mosquitoes, but Winston also knew that devouring them would keep them from biting Ellie and Benny while they were eating berries. When they finished eating, Ellie and Benny's fingers were as blue as the berries. They watched for a while as Winston darted about chasing and eating mosquitoes. Seeing that they were finished, he flew over and landed near them. As they climbed on his back, he saw their blue fingers and knew they had eaten many, many blueberries.

"Did you eat as many berries as you wanted?" Winston asked as they climbed onto his back.

"Yes," answered Benny, "and I even put some in my pocket to have when we're hungry again."

"These berries are the best of all," said Ellie. "Thank you for all the special treats. You are a good friend."

"You two are my BEST friends; I'm glad you liked the special treats," said Winston.

"Now you must hold on tightly," said Winston. "We will be flying over some really tall forest trees this time. But we will also fly past some exciting places that you MUST see."

After flying for a while, Winston saw something he knew Ellie and Benny would love to see. "If you look down to your left, I think you will be amazed." said Winston. When they looked down into the forest, what they saw was very exciting!

"Oh, look! There is the bee hive where Queenetta the Queen Bee lives," exclaimed Ellie.

"Yes, and look," said Benny. "You can see the worker bees going in and out of the hive. Could you fly down just a little closer?"

Winston did fly down closer, but only a little closer. Just as he was about to move farther on, they saw Queenetta giving something to two of the worker bees, and wave to Ellie and Benny.

The worker bees began to fly up, up, and up until they were flying right next to Winston, Ellie and Benny. They gave each of them another small comb of the Special Rainbow Forest Honey.

"Oh, yummy!" said Benny to his sister. "This one is even sweeter than the one she gave us before."

The worker bees were very busy and had to go back to work. They said goodbye as they flew back down into the forest.

Not wanting Ellie or Benny to fall or spill their honey, Winston hovered in place while his wings moved slowly. When they were finished with the honey, they also ate the berries they had left over from the blueberry fields. But no matter how much they licked their fingers, they were still covered with blue from the berries.

After telling Ellie and Benny to hold on, Winston the Dragonfly began to fly a little lower. He flew closer to the Rainbow Forest treetops.

As they were flying, Benny suddenly yelled to his sister, "Ellie, Ellie! Look down there near the tree with the purple flowers. There are butterflies that are dancing." As Ellie looked down, she saw the dancing butterflies, but she also saw something that Benny did NOT see.

"Benny, look! The butterflies are dancing on Ida-the-Spider's web and she's also dancing with them," Ellie said.

They both thought it was very funny to see the spider trying to dance. They could hardly stop laughing. They were having so much fun watching Ida dancing with the butterflies. Winston flew very slowly, so they could have a little more time to watch before moving on.

As they were flying, the forest became brighter. Winston thought he should tell Benny and Ellie what was going to happen next. Just as he was about to tell them, Ellie asked, "Why is it getting so bright?"

Before he could answer, there came a voice saying, "Hello Winston the Dragonfly! You are doing a very good job. It's good to see you back in the Rainbow Forest."

Winston smiled, and said, "Thank you. Thank you Mister Sunbeam."

Then he said to Ellie and Benny, "THAT is why it's so bright. Mister Sunbeam shines much brighter when he is very pleased."

"Why is he so pleased?" Benny asked.

"Because I've kept my promise to share, to never scare you again, and to give you special treats."

Just as he said that, he looked down to see that they were above the pond.

"Well, here we are, above the pond where I lived as an Ugly Nymph."

"Yes, but now you're a Beautiful Dragonfly, and you're our friend," said Ellie.

As Winston sailed slowly down, Ellie and Benny were surprised to see the Keeper of the Rainbow Forest waiting there. When they landed softly on the ground, they climbed off Winston's back.

"We were flying with Winston the Dragonfly," said Ellie. "He flew us to the blueberry fields."

"Yes," said Benny. "And we saw many things in the Forest while we were flying with him. We had so much fun."

"Yes, I know," said the Keeper. He then looked at Winston, and said, "You DID grow up to become a Dragonfly. Very good! You are now one of the Special Rainbow Forest Creatures. Welcome!"

"Thank you," said Winston. He then waved goodbye to his two new friends, and flew off into the forest, chasing a mosquito.

"Benny and Ellie," said the Keeper. "You both have had a very busy day."

"Yes," said Ellie. "Can you show us how to get back home?"

"We are very tired," said Benny.

"Very well," said the Keeper. But first, just sit by that boulder near the edge of the pond and rest for a little while."

They walked over and sat down by the boulder. They waved hello to their Rainbow fish friends, who were splashing about in the water. Soon they fell asleep. The Keeper of the Rainbow Forest took his Magic Sword from his silver scabbard, squeezed it three times, and sent the Crystal Sparkles sailing around them as they slept.

When Ellie and Benny woke up they were underneath the same big cherry tree in their back yard.

THE END

The inspiration for this story, two of the author's children.

ABOUT THE CREATORS

MCKENZIE WILLIS was born in Brownsville, TN. He attended Tennessee A & I State University and subsequently graduated from the State University of New York at New Paltz with a degree in Sociology. Upon graduating he was employed by the University's Research Foundation. Much of his work experience was youth/counseling oriented.

While with the New York State Education Department he delivered numerous presentations introducing educators to the department's development of a testing tool for diagnosing traumatic brain injury in youth.

McKenzie is a published song writer/lyricist and has collaborated with Saturday Night Live Music Director, L. Leon Pendarvis. One of McKenzie's published songs was recorded by blues legend Taj Mahal.

The CD of children's songs that is available as a companion to this print book is the result of a collaboration between Janice Gadsden-Pendarvis, Leon Pendarvis and McKenzie.

The inspiration for *Tales of the Rainbow Forest* was the author's two sons chasing butterflies and dragonflies in their magical backyard on Main Street in New Paltz.

RICK HOLLAND studied art, graphic design and philosophy at the State University of New York at New Paltz. His work has been published in various periodocials and books. *Tales of the Rainbow Forest* is the first children's book he has illustrated. He lives in Rosendale, NY.